HANNAH MONTANA *Insider*

Leading two lives can be tough! Miley and Lilly leave Hannah's concert early to prepare for their science test. Hannah had to turn down a date with Jesse McCartney to study earthworms. Gross! Miley wonders what it would be like to get rid of her secret, and finally live the life of a teen pop princess. When Miley and Lilly see a shooting star, Miley wishes she could be Hannah Montana all the time.

Miley's wish comes true!

Things would be so much easier! Without school taking up her time, Miley can only imagine the things she'd be able to do. No classes, no secret, no science tests—just concerts, parties, and Jesse! Miley could finally have it all: family, friends, and fame.

Ask Lulu

Now that she has it all, Hannah wants to share it with her family and friends. She can't wait to have full-time-Hannah fun with them! When Roxy takes her to the beach to see Jackson, Hannah almost doesn't recognize him. Her full-time pop star life has turned her brother into a full-time hermit. How could this happen?

When Miley became Hannah Montana, all of Jackson's friends used him to get closer to her. He couldn't trust anyone to be his friend. Jackson got tired of Hannah mania and decided to live alone on the beach. Hannah was too busy being Hannah to care.

QUIZ:
What kind of a pop star are you?

A | B

Hannah can't believe how much her family has changed now that she's a full-time pop star! Even her dad has traded in his hillbilly ways to become a Malibu man. Who will Hannah talk to now that Robby has a new wife and Jackson lives on the beach? Hannah can't wait to find Lilly and Oliver—but will they know the real Hannah from the famous Hannah?

Oliver and Lilly have totally changed! When Lilly, Oliver, and Miley were best friends, they could all be themselves. They had a blast at Seaview High together!

Because Hannah was never Miley, their friendship never existed. Instead of being themselves, Oliver and Lilly have traded in true friends for trendy cliques.

Which world would you choose?

School   Fame   Travel

Clothes   Family   Shopping

Friends   Fans

Movies

Which World?

Hannah tries to talk to Lilly. She hopes that Lilly will see past the fame and not treat Hannah any differently than she would Miley.

Best of Both Worlds

Hannah is sad and lonely after her first day without her big secret. If giving up her awesome family and wonderful friends is part of being Hannah Montana all the time, then Hannah doesn't want her wish anymore. She'll never wish to be anyone but Miley ever again!

When Hannah sees another shooting star, she wishes to go back to her double life. When she gets her wish, she can't wait to get back to her family and friends. Being a pop star isn't any fun without the people she loves the most.

It's Miley's first day at Seaview High and things couldn't be worse! Just as school begins Miley gets a mysterious text from someone who says they know her secret!

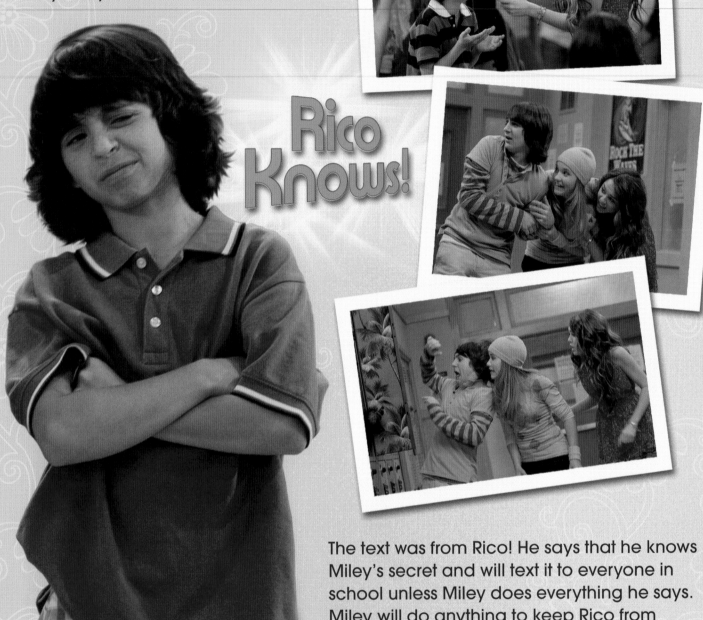

Rico Knows!

The text was from Rico! He says that he knows Miley's secret and will text it to everyone in school unless Miley does everything he says. Miley will do anything to keep Rico from telling everyone that she's Hannah Montana— even be his girlfriend for a day. But how much does Rico really know? Oliver and Lilly are on the case to get Miley off the hook!

WILL RICO TELL?

SECRET SWAP:

Match these characters to their secrets.

QUIZ: Could you keep a secret?

A | B

LILLY

• Can locate America's hottest teen pop sensation.

• Always giggles when she tells a lie.

MILEY

• Knows the real name of teen heartthrob Jake Ryan.

• Was once a pie-eating champion in Tennessee.

JACKSON

• Holds the secret to the world's best cheese jerky.

• Has a cousin named Scooby.

OLIVER

• Possesses a deep fear of chewing gum.

• Leader of the fabled Okenland.

secret POP STAR

Ms. Kunkle's Class

Gym Class

Don't sleepwalk your way into this classroom. You better hit the books if you want to pass one of Ms. Kunkle's super-hard tests!

Pick a Clique

Even though Lilly is one of the best athletes at Seaview High, she'll stick by Stinky Stewart when it's time to pick teams. That's what best friends are for!

Amber and Ashley

Miley and Lilly

Thor and Jackson

The Lockers

The lockers are where you'll find Oliver, the locker man! If you can't remember your combination, he'll be happy to work his magic.

Mr. Corelli's Class

Mr. Corelli is one of the funniest and fairest teachers around. His students can check out his web cast before class to see if he'll hand out a pop quiz.

Old Blue Jeans

Fashion Find

Trendy

Sweetheart

Pop Star

Sporty

Western

Hannah's fans love it when she appears on talk shows. They get to find out what their favorite star is up to! When Hannah goes on *The Real Deal* with Colin Lassiter, she can't wait to talk about her music.

Hannah appears with Mikayla, another teen pop sensation. Hannah and Mikayla pretend to be good friends while the cameras are rolling, but as soon as the show cuts to a commercial, Hannah finds out that Mikayla wants to wipe her off the teen scene and be the only pop princess!

QUIZ:
What kind of a talk show would you host?

A | B

After the show, Hannah discovers that Mikayla is scheduled to sing at a benefit concert in Florida. Hannah wants to perform at the same concert so that she can show Mikayla who the best pop star *really* is. Hannah can't lose any of her fans to this mean-mouthed diva—all she has to do is convince Robby to take her.

Robby agrees to take Hannah to Florida, but he decides to cancel the trip after he hurts his back. Miley begs Robby to let her go to the concert with Roxy, but Robby says Miley is too young to travel without him. Then Robby lays down the rules: if he can't go to Florida, neither can Hannah.

WhoSaid

Miley tricks Roxy into taking her. She tells Roxy that her dad *will* let her go without him. Roxy and Miley are headed to Florida! Robby finds out that Miley and Roxy are at the airport, so he goes to find them. When Miley sees Robby board the plane, she knows she's in trouble!

When Robby sits down to talk to her, Miley finds out that she's not in trouble after all. Robby agrees to let her go to Florida without him. At first, he didn't want Miley to go alone because he wants to be around to take care of her. Now Robby realizes that she's old enough to take care of herself, and she can make the trip to Florida with Roxy. Miley is so excited to go to Florida and sing Mikayla off the stage!

Hannah Montana and Mikayla are teen pop rivals. They always end up running into each other, and when they do—look out! They'll smile for the cameras when they're together, but as soon as the lights go down, their egos go up.

TRUE OR FALSE

TRUE OR FALSE

Amber and Ashley are the queen bees of Seaview High. These girls would never hang out with Miley and Lilly—unless Jake Ryan is around. How would they act if they knew Miley was really Hannah Montana?

Jackson and Rico put up with each other at the Surf Shop. Rico may be the boss, but that doesn't stop Jackson from giving Rico a taste of his own medicine. These guys pull so many pranks on each other you'd think they were in a professional practical-joke contest.

TRUE OR FALSE

VS.

Miley finds out that Lilly's new boyfriend, Lucas, has another girlfriend! She can't stand someone cheating on her best friend. Miley has to tell Lilly, even though she knows how upset her best friend will be. Lilly doesn't believe Miley when she tells her that Lucas has another girlfriend. Lilly thinks that Miley is jealous because she and Lucas have been spending so much time together.

Lilly decides to find Miley a boyfriend of her own, and brings Lucas's cousin to movie night.

Lilly needs to know the truth! Miley thinks of a plan to catch Lucas. She decides to send Oliver undercover. If Lilly won't believe Miley, maybe she'll believe a video.

Miley comes up with another idea. Lucas definitely won't tell Lilly that he has another girlfriend, but maybe he'll tell Lola. It's time for Hannah and Lola to have a night out on the town!

Who has a crush on Lilly?

Miley finds the new song Robby has written for Hannah. She can't believe her award-winning, songwriting dad has written such awful lyrics! Hannah could never sing this song for her fans. How can she tell her dad that she hates it?

QUIZ: Can you keep your cool?

A | B

Miley knows she should tell Robby the truth, but she doesn't want to hurt his feelings. He's excited about the song! She'll have to pretend to really like whatever he plays for her. Miley is so nervous about lying to her dad that she starts to walk and talk in her sleep!

Jackson is nervous, too. He hears Miley talking about Robby's bad song in her sleep. If Robby hears what Miley says about his new song, then he'll be in a bad mood. Jackson wants to keep Robby's spirits up so he can throw a party over the weekend. Jackson decides to keep Miley from sleepwalking, no matter what it takes!

Miley finally decides to tell Robby that she doesn't like the new song. It turns out the song she found wasn't the song that Robby had written for Hannah. Instead, it was a song that Miley had written when she was little! Robby says that he always keeps that song in his pocket for inspiration, and to make him giggle.

The Other Side of Me

Write your own crazy song.

letter	Beijing	speedy
sweater	Memphis	weepy
wrench	Paris	happy

PLAY

ROUND 1

Jackson and Miley bust the pipes in Jackson's bathroom while playing pranks on each other. As Miley and Jackson fight over who is at fault, their sibling spat moves to the next level when they begin to insult each other. Robby is tired of their fighting and decides to make them share Miley's bathroom until Jackson's can be fixed. Robby hopes that Miley and Jackson will learn to get along if they have to share something they both need.

ROUND 2

Sharing a bathroom is a lot harder than Jackson and Miley thought it would be. Jackson's stuff is everywhere and he's using all of her things! Robby can't stand that Miley and Jackson are fighting more now than they did before. What else can he do to make Miley and Jackson get along and be friends? What would Uncle Earl do?

ROUND 3

Robby decides to let Miley and Jackson resolve their problems in Sumo suits. This way, they can let out their anger and start to have fun together. Instead, Miley and Jackson continue to fight as they knock each other to the ground! Robby gives up. He doesn't know how to keep them from fighting.

Later that night, Jackson's car gets stuck. Hannah and Jackson are forced to stop fighting and help each other out of the car. Once they are both out of the car safely, they realize how important they are to each other and their sibling freeze-out ends. It took a long time, but they finally realize what a dynamic duo they are!

QUIZ:
Who are you like?

A | B

MILEY OR JACKSON:
Who would you choose?

TRUE OR FALSE

Hannah receives an International Music Award! Aunt Dolly and Mamaw have both made it to Malibu for the occasion. Hannah is so happy they will be there when she takes the stage.

We Got the Party

Hannah has always wanted her own Booty, and now she has one! Just like her dad, Hannah accepts a Silver Boot Award. It's a great honor for this Tennessee girl to receive an award for the best country/pop crossover.

QUIZ:
How much do you know about Hannah's career?

A | B | C